WHOLE WORLD

For my sister, Liz — C. C.

Barefoot Books
124 Walcot Street
Bath, BA1 5BG

Barefoot Books
2067 Massachusetts Ave
Cambridge, MA 02140

First published in Great Britain by Barefoot Books Ltd and in the United States of America
by Barefoot Books, Inc. in 2007. This paperback edition published in 2009

Illustrations copyright © 2007 by Christopher Corr
The moral right of Christopher Corr to be identified as the
illustrator of this work has been asserted

This book has been printed on 100% acid-free paper

Graphic design by Penny Lamprell, Lymington, England
Reproduction by Grafiscan, Verona
Printed and bound in China by Printplus Ltd

This book was typeset in Kosmik and ChildsPlay
The illustrations were prepared in gouache on Fabriano paper

Paperback ISBN 978-1-84686-424-7

British Cataloguing-in-Publication Data:
a catalogue record for this book is available from the British Library

135798642

The Library of Congress cataloged the hardcover edition as follows:

Corr, Christopher.
  Whole world / Christopher Corr.
    p. cm.
  Summary: An illustrated version of the well-known song, featuring the relationship between people
and the natural world.
  ISBN-13: 978-1-84686-043-0 (hardcover : alk. paper)
  1. Spirituals (Songs)—Texts. 2. Children's songs, English—United States—Texts.
[1. Spirituals (Songs) 2. Songs.] I. He's got the whole world in his hands. II. Title.
  PZ8.3.C81882Who 2007
  782.42—dc22
  [E]

                                                              2006023455

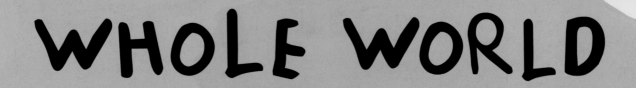

WHOLE WORLD

Illustrated by Christopher Corr

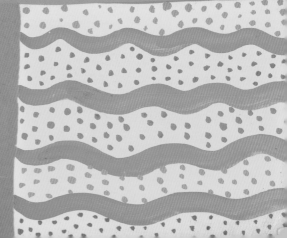

Barefoot Books
Celebrating Art and Story

We've got the whole world in our hands,
We've got the whole world in our hands,

We've got the whole world in our hands,
We've got the whole world in our hands!

She's got the sun and the moon in her hands,

She's got the sun and the moon in her hands,

She's got the sun and the moon in her hands,

She's got the whole world in her hands!

He's got the mountains and the valleys in his hands,

He's got the mountains and the valleys in his hands,

He's got the mountains and the valleys in his hands,

He's got the whole world in his hands!

She's got the plains and the deserts in her hands,
She's got the plains and the deserts in her hands,

She's got the plains and the deserts in her hands,
She's got the whole world in her hands!

He's got the lakes and the rivers in his hands,
He's got the lakes and the rivers in his hands,

He's got the lakes and the rivers in his hands,
He's got the whole world in his hands!

She's got the trees and the flowers in her hands,
She's got the trees and the flowers in her hands,

She's got the fish of the sea in her hands,

She's got the fish of the sea in her hands,

She's got the fish of the sea in her hands,

She's got the whole world in her hands!

He's got the towns and the cities in his hands,
He's got the towns and the cities in his hands,

He's got the towns and the cities in his hands,
He's got the whole world in his hands!

We've got the whole world in our hands,
We've got the whole world in our hands,

We've got the whole world in our hands,
We've got the whole world in our hands!

Did You Know?

We really do have the whole world in our hands — it is up to us to take care of it!

Here is some information about the creatures and environments in this book:

Sun

Almost all of the earth's energy comes from the sun — without the sun, the earth would be a big block of ice! People have depended on the sun for as long as there has been life on earth, for lots of different reasons. The sun has always been very important to farmers, because the crops need its light. In ancient times, the movements of the sun were used for telling the time and setting apart the different seasons.

Moon

The moon is at its brightest in our night sky, after the sun has set. Farmers and gardeners often depend on the moon to know when to plant new seeds, and ocean tides are controlled by the pull of the moon. There are lots of moon festivals all over the world, where people celebrate its wonder. Air pollution is changing our view of the moon — smog makes the sky look thick, foggy and dark, which blocks the moon from our sight.

Mountains

The great mountain ranges of the world were created millions of years ago by pressure caused when tectonic plates — sections of the earth's surface — pushed up against each other. Mountains have historically formed natural boundaries between different countries because they are difficult or impossible to pass, especially in winter. Many mountains that have been snow-capped for centuries are now changing, as global warming raises temperatures and the snowcaps melt.

Valleys

Valleys are the lowlands between mountains. Many of the world's valleys were created at the end of the Ice Age, when the glaciers melted. Valleys often have very rich soil, so they are areas where farming communities have regularly settled. In just a spoonful of this soil, there can be a billion living things, such as worms and seeds. Valleys also offer protection from severe weather, and are used as trading routes.

Plains

Plains are large areas of flat, open land, such as savannahs and tundra. Animals like cheetahs and zebras live on savannahs, while, in fertile areas, plains are used for farming. Plains exist all over the world, from North America to Spain to Iran, but many of them are becoming polluted. As rain falls and trickles down the land, it picks up any pollutants as it goes. These then settle in the low plains.

Deserts

Deserts are dry lands, and can be either very hot or very cold. Some deserts have no rain for years and years! Deserts may seem like places without life, but lots of living things make their homes there, such as bats, birds, frogs, lizards, plants, snakes and even fish. The lives of these plants and animals are all connected — they depend on each other for survival.

Ways to Reduce Global Warming

Global warming is caused by carbon dioxide that is released into the atmosphere. There are lots of different causes for this, such as cars and planes. Global warming causes temperature and climate changes that affect every living thing on earth. There are some simple things that everyone can do to help reduce global warming:

- Don't fly or drive if you don't have to. Take the bus or the train, walk, run or cycle!

- Use renewable energy — that means power from wind or solar energy, from the sun.

- Recycle! This dramatically reduces the amount of waste in our environment.

- Use less hot water. It takes a lot of energy to heat up water.

- Turn off and unplug your TV, stereo and computer when you're not using them.

- Hang your clothes outside to dry instead of using the tumble dryer.

- Use recycled paper to save trees from being cut down.

- Eat less meat. Forests full of trees that reduce carbon dioxide in the air are cut down to make way for cows that will be used for food.

- Buy local and organic food. This means less fuel is being used to transport the food to you.

- Replace old light bulbs with compact fluorescent bulbs — these use 60 per cent less energy than regular bulbs.

- Plant a tree — it will absorb one ton of carbon dioxide in its lifetime.

Sing Along

The original version of this song was written by African American pianist and composer, Margaret Bonds (1913-1972). "He's Got the Whole World in His Hands" is very well known as a gospel spiritual.

We've got the whole world _____ in our_ hands, We've got the whole_____ world_____

in our_ hands, We've got the whole world _____ in our_ hands, We've got the whole world in our hands!_____

She's got the sun and the moon in her hands . . .

He's got the mountains and the valleys in his hands . . .

She's got the plains and the deserts in her hands . . .

He's got the lakes and the rivers in his hands . . .

She's got the trees and the flowers in her hands . . .

He's got the birds of the air in his hands . . .

She's got the fish of the sea in her hands . . .

He's got the towns and the cities in his hands . . .

Repeat first verse!